Weird Happenings

by

Kaye Umansky

Illustrated by Chris Mould

Read more about the Weird family in the first book in the series, *Meet the Weirds*, also available from Barrington Stoke:
www.barringtonstoke.co.uk

First published in 2004 in Great Britain by
Barrington Stoke Ltd
18 Walker Street, Edinburgh, EH3 7LP

www.barringtonstoke.co.uk

Reprinted 2005, 2008, 2009

ISBN: 978-1-84299-207-4

Printed in Great Britain by Bell & Bain Ltd

When Chris met Kaye ... the illustrator asks the author some questions

Where do your characters come from ... are they people you know?

The people in my stories are all made up. Once I've made them up, they speak for themselves. They live in my mind and they say what that sort of person would say.

Do you ever dream your stories in your sleep?

I do dream about writing in my sleep, most of all if I get stuck. I have horrible nightmares! Don't get me wrong, though. Writing is fun!

What was the naughtiest thing you did at school?!

I'm not telling. It's too awful.

When Kaye met Chris ... the author asks the illustrator some questions

What was your favourite book when you were a kid?

The Tyger Voyage by Richard Adams, illustrated by Nicola Bayley. It made me want to draw when I was only a young lad! My father bought it for me and it still sits in my window.

Where do you work?

At the top of the house in a darkened room under a pile of books and papers.

Who's the weirdest person you know?!

We're all a bit weird up here in Yorkshire. I'd better choose myself, just to be on the safe side! My mum says I'm "DIFFERENT". I think she's being polite.

To my long-suffering family

Contents

1 Trouble at Breakfast   1

2 The Weirds Next Door   11

3 An Accident   27

4 Upstairs   37

5 The Forbidden Loft   43

6 Help!   53

7 The Primms Return   65

Chapter 1
Trouble at Breakfast

It was Saturday morning. Pinchton Primm sat at the breakfast table, eating a bowl of sawdust and rabbit droppings.

"More healthy Bran-o-Flakes, darling? Make you grow big and strong!" asked his mother, sipping tea.

"No thank you, Mother," said Pinchton. "I'm full now."

1

From outside came the roaring sound of a Harley-Davidson motorbike starting up. Mrs Primm made a face and said, "I *do* wish Isa would get rid of that bike. Why can't she get a nice little family car, like normal people?"

"Oh, I don't know." Pinchton's father spoke from behind his morning paper. He sounded quite dreamy. "Takes me back, that sound. Wind in my hair. The open road."

Mr Primm was a deputy bank manager who always wore suits and didn't have much hair for the wind to get in. But just a few days ago, Mr Primm had told Pinchton that *he* had once had a motorbike, a long time ago, before he married Mrs Primm. When he got married, Mrs Primm had made him sell it.

Pinchton was still feeling shocked. It was like finding out that his father had been a member of the Moon landing team or a singer in a rock band.

"Did you hear the noises again last night? From next door?" tutted Mrs Primm. "The songs? The laughter? All the bangs and crashes? I didn't sleep a wink."

"I wonder where my old leather jacket is?" Mr Primm went on. He was still thinking about his motorbike. He saw himself speeding down the open road. He wasn't listening to Mrs Primm at all.

"I shall have to have another word with the people next door," she said. "This can't go on."

"You didn't throw it away, did you?" Mr Primm asked his wife.

"I really have no idea, Rodney. Now, Pinchton, fold your napkin if you've finished eating. Must I remind you again?"

"Sorry, Mother," said Pinchton, and folded his napkin.

"You see? That wasn't hard, was it? Now, off you go and put your best shirt on. We're going in ten minutes."

"What?" said Pinchton, startled. "Going where?"

"Oh, Pinchton!" cried Mrs Primm. "Don't say you've forgotten. Lunch! At Aunty's!"

Pinchton's heart sank. Of course. On the last Saturday of the month, they always visited his Aunty Sue and Uncle Brian who lived in a bungalow full of china and frilly curtains on the edge of a village where nothing ever happened. They had small, creepy twin daughters called Amy and May who wore matching clothes and hardly ever spoke. They *never* spoke to Pinchton.

The trip to their house was always the same. Pinchton and his parents always had to drive for hours to get there. They always stopped at a motorway service station to get flowers and Pinchton's parents would always argue about what to buy. Then, every time, they would drive off and miss the turning to Aunty Sue's village and blame Pinchton for failing to warn them in time.

When they reached the bungalow, there was always kissing and cups of tea. Pinchton would sit on the edge of a slippery sofa, trying not to yawn while the grown-ups talked and the twins stared.

For lunch, there would be salad.

Afterwards, they would all go for a stroll around the village and admire the hanging baskets. They would visit a garden centre. Then they would go back to the bungalow and listen to the twins playing *London's Burning* on their recorders until it was time to go home.

"I'm ... er ... I'm afraid I can't come this time," said Pinchton. "Didn't I tell you? There's a ... thing at school." He blushed and fiddled with his napkin. He wasn't good at lying.

"Thing? What *thing*?" demanded his mother sharply.

"I don't know, a jumble sale or something. I said I'd help sort the stuff," lied Pinchton.

"Do you hear that, Rodney? Pinchton's made arrangements to help at some *jumble* thing."

"I was fond of that jacket," said Mr Primm, unhelpfully.

"Why didn't you say, Pinchton?" said Mrs Primm crossly. "It's very selfish of you. Aunty Sue will have lunch ready and everything. And the girls will be *so* upset."

Pinchton thought about his spooky cousins and said nothing.

"So what time is this *jumble* thing?" went on his mother. "I suppose we could leave a little later if—"

"Ten o'clock," lied Pinchton. "I said I'd help sell, too. I'll be ages. And I've got loads of homework. It's all right, you go without me. I'll be fine."

"But what about your lunch?"

"I'll make myself a lettuce sandwich. You go. Really."

"Hmm," said Mrs Primm. "Are you listening, Rodney? What do you think?"

"What?" said Mr Primm.

"Pinchton says he'll stay on his own."

"The boy's old enough to look after himself, my dear," said Mr Primm. He sighed and folded his newspaper. "What's he going to do? Cut his foot off? Trash the place?"

"Ha, ha," laughed Pinchton, to make his dad happy. "As if, ha, ha."

"Well, all right," said his mother, grumpily. "I suppose we can leave Pinchton here. But I'm not happy with you, Pinchton. You should have told us before."

"I know. Sorry."

"Just remember your key. And double-lock the door. Use the brown seedy loaf and don't cut yourself when you're making your sandwich. Make sure you rinse the lettuce.

And wash your hands well afterwards if you've been handling dirty old clothes ..."

There was a lot more of the same. Pinchton nodded and said *yes* and *no* in all the right places. He promised not to eat ice cream from vans or drink dirty water or pass out in the shower. He promised to take his shoes off if he went into the lounge, because of the cream carpet. Then he helpfully offered to load the dishwasher while his parents got ready to go to Aunty Sue's.

At last, they were off. Pinchton waved goodbye at the front door as they pulled away. He waited five minutes, just in case they had forgotten something and came back.

Then he raced upstairs, changed into his football strip, and went to visit the Weirds.

Chapter 2
The Weirds Next Door

The Weirds lived next door. They had moved into Number 17, Tidy Street, a few weeks ago and Pinchton had made friends with them. There were six people in the family. All of them were – well, weird.

Otterly was the one Pinchton met first. Otterly Weird. Ott for short. She was about his age. She wore strange clothes and liked climbing trees and making dens. As far as

Pinchton could tell, she lived on sweets and *nobody even cared!* All the Weirds had odd eating habits. The only thing they all seemed to like was chips.

Then there was Oliver, Ott's brother. He was very tall and liked doing homework, even when he didn't have to! He liked eating wedding cake and had the messiest

12

room on this planet, but *nobody told him off.*

Pinchton found that amazing. *He* got into trouble if he had an untidy waste paper bin.

The baby was called Frankly Weird. He spent his time trailing around in a droopy nappy, doing annoying baby things. He took stuff and broke stuff and touched stuff he shouldn't. He had done some terrible things in Pinchton's garden, but that's another story.

Then there were the grown-ups. There was Gran, who only came up to Pinchton's shoulder. She knew all about star signs and fortune-telling and stuff. She always wore black and lived in the kitchen, frying chips over an open fire.

Mr Weird was an inventor with mad-scientist hair. Pinchton wasn't sure what his first name was. He thought he'd heard Mrs Weird call him Dead, but that wasn't right, surely? Anyway, he hardly ever came up from the cellar. Pinchton had never been down there and wasn't sure he wanted to. There were nightly bangs and horrible smells.

Mrs Weird (Isa) was a stunt woman. She was always off skydiving or grappling with sharks. She dyed her hair a bright orange, wore a lot of lipstick and strode around in pink cowboy boots, eating chicken drumsticks.

Then there were the pets. The black cat, called Ginger. The House Plant – an odd life form with stalks which lived in a pot in the kitchen and *swayed* at you when you walked by. Pinchton had seen it with his own eyes. (Unless he was going mad.)

Last of all, there was the strange Thudding Thing which lived somewhere deep in the house and kicked up a fearful racket whenever visitors called. Pinchton still hadn't found out what *that* was.

He stood on the Weirds' front doorstep and knocked gently on the faded door.

Right on cue, the Thudding Thing
started up from inside the house. There
came the distant sounds of violent
thumping and splintering wood.

Pinchton waited, breathing in the faint
smell of motorbike fumes. Nobody had
tidied up the front garden, he noticed.
It was still full of old packing cases and
cardboard boxes. A supermarket trolley lay
rusting away under a bush.

He heard heavy, clumping footsteps.
The door opened and there stood Ott,
wearing a green woolly bobble hat, a blue
net dress and a battered pair of ice skates.
It seemed an odd choice of clothing for a
Saturday morning.

"Hi," she said. "Come on in. We're in the
kitchen."

"What are you dressed up as?" asked Pinchton, politely.

"I'm not *dressed up* as anything. These are my clothes."

She clumped off on her skates, wobbling a bit. Pinchton stepped in. The Thudding Thing was silent now, he noticed. He really must ask about that.

He followed her down the long, dark hall. Past the bikes, the scooters, the coats, the boots, the suit of armour, the motorbike parts, the harp, the stepladder, the totem pole, the spinning wheel, the scuba-diving gear, the grand piano and the piles of newspaper. Past the stuffed fox, the sacks of potatoes, the giant jars of cooking oil and the picture of the mad-looking camel. A bare Christmas tree sat in a bucket. Christmas was ages ago. Had they brought it with them? Didn't the Weirds *ever* throw anything away?

Pinchton thought of the hall in his house, with its polished floorboards, silver-framed wedding photos, cream rugs and single vase of tasteful dried grass.

As he walked into the kitchen, the smell was the same as last time. Gran was tipping the latest batch of chips out onto sheets of newspaper spread out on the floor. There was no sign of the cat, but the House Plant was in its usual place on the table. It had grown since Pinchton's last visit. It waggled its stalks at him in a hopeful way, as if it wanted Pinchton to play.

Pinchton kept well out of its way.

"It's Pinch," said Ott to Gran.

Gran stared darkly into Pinchton's face and said, "It's your unlucky day."

"Is it?" said Pinchton.

"Yep. If I was you, I'd go back to bed right now."

"But I've only just got up," said Pinchton.

"The stars don't lie. Be warned. Stay away from green and beware of ladders. Have a chip."

"Thanks," said Pinchton and took one. He loved chips. They never had them at home.

Frankly sat in a corner with a bowl of pink custard. His chosen outfit of the day was a nappy, tastefully teamed with a Batman cape, hamster slippers and a blue bead necklace.

"Hello, Frankly," said Pinchton. "Are you being a good boy?"

Frankly gave him a hard stare, then turned his bowl upside down onto his own head. There was nothing to say to that.

Pinchton stared around the kitchen. It reminded him of a campsite, what with the fire and the sizzling pan and nowhere to sit.

"Where is everyone today?" he asked.

"Mum left early, to dive in arctic waters," explained Ott. "Dad's in the cellar, can't be disturbed. And Oliver's up in his room, trying to find his shoes. They've been lost for days."

Pinchton wasn't surprised. Oliver's room, he knew, was a black hole. His shoes had probably been sucked into another universe.

"You got out of seeing yer cousins, then," said Gran, suddenly. She winked at Pinchton.

Pinchton was startled. How did she know? Had his mother said something to her? He doubted it.

Just then, Oliver sloped into the room, wearing his pyjamas and carrying a banjo with two broken strings. He was so tall, his pyjama legs ended just below his knees. His head just missed bumping the light bulb.

"Found your shoes?" asked Gran.

"No," said Oliver, helping himself to chips. "But I found this banjo in my filing cabinet."

"Lovely," said Gran, smiling at him. "Give us a tune, then."

Oliver perched on the kitchen table and strummed the strings. The House Plant reached out a tendril and gently stroked his neck. Anyway, it looked that way.

"Was it filed under B for Banjo?" asked Pinchton.

"No," said Oliver. "S for Shoes."

"Perhaps your shoes are under B, then?" Pinchton said, helpfully.

"Possibly," said Oliver, twanging away.

Frankly suddenly got to his feet and began to jump about and sing. He sang very loudly and in a flat voice. He still had the custard bowl upside down on his head. Globs of pink goo ran down his face. Ott giggled.

"That's it, Frankly, you dance," said Gran, nodding happily.

"Boop, boop," sang Frankly, kicking up his hamster slippers. "Boopy boop boop!"

"What a lovely song," said Ott. "How does it go again?"

"BOOOP!" bellowed Frankly. "BOOOOOP!"

Nobody paid any attention. Gran threw some more chips into the pan. Oliver carried on strumming. The Plant began swaying in time to the music. Of course, it could have been a breeze that made it sway.

Although the window was shut.

"So what do you fancy doing today?" shouted Ott, over the horrible noise.

"Don't mind," yelled Pinchton.

"BOOOP!"

"How long can you stay?"

"All day. My parents are out."

"BOOOOP!"

"Really? Can we come and see your house?"

"Er ..." Pinchton trailed off. This was tricky. He didn't want to sound unfriendly, but somehow he didn't think his parents would like him to have visitors.

"We won't stay long," went on Ott. "We just want to see your room. Don't we, Oliver?"

"What?" said Oliver.

"Pinch has invited us to his house. You want to come, don't you?"

"All right," said Oliver.

"I'm not sure ..." began poor Pinchton, but no one heard him.

"*BOOOOOOOOP!!*"

"Take Frankly with you," said Gran. "He'd enjoy that."

Hmmm.

Chapter 3
An Accident

"Would you like a drink or something?" asked Pinchton. He wanted to be the perfect host. He didn't often have friends back. It was too embarrassing when his mother made them take their shoes off.

The Weirds waited in the kitchen doorway. Ott had changed out of her ice skates, thank goodness. Pinchton hated to think what they might have done to the shiny floorboards in the hall. She had wanted to go into the lounge but Pinchton had hurried on by. At least the kitchen was a carpet-free zone. He could wipe up any mess they made on the floor.

"Wow!" said Ott. Her mouth dropped open as she looked at the gleaming and spotless kitchen. "It's so *clean.* Look, Frankly. Isn't it clean?"

Frankly was struck dumb by how clean everything was. He simply stood and hugged his custard bowl, eyes goggling.

"I know," said Pinchton, sadly. He wished he hadn't cleared away the breakfast things now.

"Not like ours at all," went on Ott. "You could eat off the floor in this kitchen."

"I know," sighed Pinchton, and hung his head.

"We *do* eat off the floor in our kitchen," pointed out Oliver. "But I expect we shouldn't," he added.

"So, what do you want?" asked Pinchton again.

"What have you got?" asked Ott.

Pinchton opened the fridge door and, as always, was dazzled by green. Everything, on the shelves, in the door, was green.

"There's spinach juice – or grape juice with bits in," he said. "Or filtered water. Or my mother's homemade celery drink, but I wouldn't have that if I was you."

"I'll pass, thanks," said Ott.

"What about you, Oliver?" asked Pinchton. Oliver was still hovering in the doorway, peering through his owlish glasses. His feet were still bare, but he had pulled an anorak over his pyjamas.

"Have you got any wedding cake?" asked Oliver.

"No. Sorry."

"What did you say you've got again?"

"Come on over and have a look," invited Pinchton.

"Right," said Oliver. He took one step into the room. One step, that's all.

Boing!

The top of his head crashed into a hanging basket of pink pansies which Pinchton's mother had bought only the day before. The basket swung up, jerked off its hook, and to Pinchton's horror, fell like a stone.

Crash! Earth, broken pottery, pink petals and bits of plant were everywhere.

All over the tiles. In the corners. Under the table. Everywhere.

There was a stunned silence.

"Was that me?" said Oliver. "Sorry."

"Trust you, Oliver," said Ott, with a little giggle.

Most toddlers would have cried with fright at all the noise. Not Frankly. Frankly started to smile. He pulled up his nappy, sat down on the floor and briskly began filling his custard bowl with earth.

"That's it, Frankly, you dig," said Ott.

"No!" cried Pinchton. "No, don't dig!"

"What's the matter?" said Ott. "It was only an accident. Will your mum be cross?"

"It's all right," said Pinchton. He wanted to be polite. After all, they were guests. "It's all right, it's nothing, I'll clean it up, it's all right. Just stop Frankly getting mud everywhere, will you? I'll get the dustpan, it's all right."

He fled to the cupboard where his mother kept the cleaning things. He jerked it open and a load of saucepans came crashing out onto the floor. Wrong cupboard. He went for the next one.

"I can't find it!" he wailed, poking around. A million wire scrubbing things slithered out. A bottle of green liquid overturned. The top came off. Slimy green cleaning stuff globbed out.

"Don't panic! We'll help!" shouted Ott. "Come on, Oliver!"

From behind came the sound of cupboard doors quickly opening and closing. More stuff was falling out onto the floor.

"No, don't!" yelled Pinchton, scrabbling madly at the back of another cupboard. "Don't help! I'll find it! I know where things are! Just don't – ah, here it is!"

He crawled out of the cupboard, waving the brush and dustpan. At last.

But it was too late. Things had gone beyond the sweeping stage.

Frankly had found the sink. He was on a chair. He had turned on the tap and was busily adding water to the mess on the tiles.

The kitchen floor was now one huge pool of mud.

"The mop!" wailed Pinchton, wringing his hands. "I have to find the mop!"

"Tell you what," said Ott. "Let's not bother cleaning up right now. Let's do it later. Let's see your room. Upstairs, yes?"

"And leave this mess? Are you mad?" squeaked Pinchton.

But he was talking to empty air.

Chapter 4
Upstairs

"Cor," said Ott. "It's very ... *serious*, isn't it?"

They were clustered in the doorway. Frankly was hanging back a bit, sucking his thumb, unsure again.

"Yes. Well, you've seen it, so that's that," said Pinchton. "Look, I really think I should go down and deal with the kitchen."

He didn't like showing them his room. It was perfectly tidy, as always. His clothes were put away, bed made, books in neat order from A-Z. All there was on his desk was a pen and new, clean pad of paper neatly headed *Homework* with nothing written on it. In pride of place sat the PlayStation 2 he so loved, which his Uncle Ted had given him so his parents couldn't say anything.

Oliver's eyes fell on the empty pad and lit up.

"Wow! Homework! What have you got to do?"

"Write a story about being a Roman gladiator," sighed Pinchton.

"Great. I'll do it." Oliver folded himself into Pinchton's chair, grabbed the pen and instantly began to write.

"He will," agreed Ott, as the first page began to fill up with Oliver's spidery writing. "He's very good."

"But Miss'll know it's not my handwriting."

"So copy it out. Go on, let him. Look how happy he is."

Oliver was on his second page and didn't even look up.

"Well ... all right," said Pinchton. "Thanks. Look, I'm going down to find the mop."

"What's the rush?" said Ott. She began wandering around Pinchton's perfect room, picking things up and putting them back in all the wrong places. Frankly had got over his shyness and was now bouncing up and down on Pinchton's bed, leaving dirty smears all over the duvet.

"Because there's a muddy lake in the kitchen!" snapped Pinchton. "A muddy lake with our saucepans floating in it.
My parents will go mad!"

"No, they won't. Relax. We've got all day to clear it up."

"That's all very well for you to say," said Pinchton, rather stiffly. "My mother's fussy about tidiness and things."

"Trust me, I'll get it sorted," said Ott, carelessly. "Aren't there any *untidy* rooms in your house?"

"No," confessed Pinchton. He took a deep breath and tried to relax. Well, he did have all day. His parents wouldn't arrive home until six at the earliest. There was plenty of time to clean the kitchen and get rid of the mess. He could take the savings from his money box and nip along to the flower shop and get another hanging basket and hope nobody noticed. And Oliver was doing his homework for him. Perhaps all wasn't lost.

"So where do you keep all your stuff?" went on Ott.

"Stuff?"

"You know. Old photos and suitcases and broken beds and chairs."

"I don't think we have any. Unless it's up in the loft."

At once, he wished he hadn't said that.

"The loft?" said Ott.

"Yes, I've never been up there."

"Hear that, Oliver? Pinchton's got a loft and he's never been up there."

"I'm not allowed," said Pinchton. "The floor's unsafe."

Oliver looked up from writing. Ott stared at him. Together, they both said, "So?"

Chapter 5
The Forbidden Loft

"Be careful," warned Pinchton. "The floor's unsafe up here."

"We know," said Oliver. "You said."

The forbidden loft was reached by a pull-down stepladder leading to a trap door.

They stood in stuffy darkness, peering around. There was a switch on the wall to the right of the trap door. Ott pressed it and a single bulb came on, sending shadows hurrying away into far corners.

"You see?" she said. "I knew it would be interesting."

It was. The low roof had bare beams sloping down to the floor. The floor was made of flimsy old planks laid carelessly any old how. No one had been up here in a long time. Everything was draped in cobwebs.

All around the edges were great piles of stuff. Stuff Pinchton never knew they had. Boxes and crates full of old books and ugly pictures. Broken chairs and tables. A dartboard. A tailor's dummy. An old-fashioned sewing machine. Dusty suitcases. A roll of moth-eaten carpet. A huge pile of old *Biker* magazines.

"Well, that's it," said Pinchton. "I think we'd better go down now – hey! What are you doing?"

All three Weirds had spread out to the far corners of the loft and were poking about in the boxes. The planks creaked as they moved around. It didn't sound good.

"Careful," warned Pinchton, anxiously. "The boards aren't safe."

"We know," said Oliver, busy looking through a box of books. "You keep saying."

Ott was on her knees in front of an old chest, fiddling with the lock. Frankly had found the sewing machine and was happily turning the handle.

"Look," said Pinchton, "I really think we should go down now."

"Why?" said Ott. "It's good up here. It's the best place in the house."

"It's dangerous. Frankly's about to sew his foot, and the ..."

"... boards aren't safe, yes, you said. Oh, *bother* this lock."

"Hey, look!" said Oliver. "Here's an old photo album. Is that your dad?"

Moving with care, Pinchton edged slowly across to join him. He looked down at where Oliver was pointing. The photo was a bit blurred around the edges, but it was of his father, and no mistake. His father with – *arrrrrgh!* – long hair. Long, *wavy* hair. Sitting astride a motorbike, wearing ugly platform boots and a fringed leather jacket with zips.

"Look at that," said Pinchton, with a little whistle. "Look at the boots. Look at that *hair.* Why did they do that, back in the old days?"

He turned the page. On the other side was a heart-shaped photo of his mother looking sweetly girlish in what was clearly her best dress. The next photo was of them both, standing together in a neat garden. His mother had his father firmly by the arm. He was wearing a suit and he'd had a haircut. No sign of the bike.

Pinchton looked back at the bike photo.

"That must be the jacket he was talking about this morning."

"You mean *this* jacket?" said Ott, over by the chest. At last, she had got it open. She held up a black, stiff-looking garment with fringes hanging down and a lot of zips.

"That's it!" cried Pinchton. "It wasn't thrown out after all!"

"Horrible style, isn't it?" said Ott. "Smells funny, too."

"Still," said Pinchton, "my father likes it. I think it reminds him of when he was young."

Excited, he took a step towards it.

Forgetting all about the floorboards.

There was a sharp crack. A thick cloud of dirty white plaster dust rose up into the air. With a little cry, Pinchton fell forward, landing painfully on his hands and one knee.

He looked for his other knee. It was gone. His entire leg had vanished through a gaping hole in the floor and was currently dangling from the ceiling of the room below.

Which was his parent's bedroom.

There was a terrible silence. Then, "Again!" shouted Frankly, clapping his hands.

"Wow!" said Ott, swiping the dust out of her streaming eyes. "Are you all right, Pinch?"

"Mind out for the floorboards," suggested Oliver, helpfully. "They're not safe."

"What have I done? Oh, what have I done?" groaned Pinchton, slowly pulling his leg back up through the hole. It was covered in plaster dust up to the knee, but at least it still moved. Thankfully there wasn't any blood or anything. Pinchton wasn't good with blood.

The four of them peered down. Chunks of plaster were scattered over the snowy white bedspread below. More lay on the cream carpet. Dust was settling thickly on the polished wooden dressing table. Several photos had been knocked off the bedside table and lay on the floor, the broken glass in splinters beside them.

"Tell you what," said Ott. "Let's go and have a word with Gran."

Chapter 6
Help!

"Guess what, Gran?" said Ott, as she came into the Weirds' kitchen. Pinchton was close behind her. He was in a real panic.

Gran was in the middle of watering the House Plant, which seemed to be enjoying it, stretching its stalks in a cheerful sort of way.

"What?" said Gran.

"Pinchton has the cleanest house in the universe. Everything smells of lemons and the fridge is full of bottled grass and—"

"Never mind about that!" howled Pinchton. "Tell her what's happened!"

"Oh. Right. Well, we had a couple of accidents."

"What sort of accidents?" said Gran.

"Mud pool in the kitchen and a hole in a ceiling," said Oliver, loping in with Frankly. "Nothing major."

He perched on the table, picked up his banjo and began to play it.

"Nothing *major*?" spluttered Pinchton. "Nothing *major*? What does *major* mean for you, then?"

"When you wake up in the morning and find your house has vanished down a hole in your garden," said Oliver.

"Oh, yes," sneered Pinchton. "A likely story. Whenever has *that* happened?"

"It happened to us," said Ott. "That's why we moved here. Things always happen to our houses."

"They either slowly crumble around our ears," nodded Oliver, "or Dad blows them up."

"Bless him," added Gran, fondly. "He'll be wanting his chips soon."

"A hole in the ceiling's nothing," explained Ott. "That's all we're saying. It could be a lot worse."

"It could? How? Oh, wait. I suppose nobody set fire to the lounge," snapped

Pinchton sarcastically. "We'll go back and do that right now, shall we? Anyone got any matches?"

"What's the yelling about?" boomed a breezy new voice, and Mrs Weird came striding into the kitchen in her biker gear. She threw down her helmet, shook out her orange hair, scooped up Frankly, set him down in the sink and turned the tap on before kicking off her pink boots and helping herself to a chip.

"Hello, Mrs Weird," said Pinchton. "Sorry. I'm a bit upset, that's all."

"That's okay, yell away. Yell whenever you want. I do."

"Thanks."

"Yell again now if you like," offered Mrs Weird, kindly. "Don't be shy. I'll join you."

"No, really, I'm fine. How was diving in arctic waters?"

"Cold. Did I hear something about a hole in a ceiling?"

"Yes!" cried Pinchton, feeling better because, at last, someone seemed to understand why he was so worried. "Yes, that's exactly it."

Mrs Weird reached for her handbag, took out a mirror, leaned on the table and began applying orange lipstick. The House Plant seemed to snuggle up. But maybe that was just Pinchton's crazy state of mind.

"Just the one hole?" she asked, smacking her lips together.

"Yes. But there's a mud pool in the kitchen, too, and a terrible mess in my parents' room and I have to get a new hanging basket and—"

58

"When are they back?"

"Um – probably about six."

"Ah, relax, plenty of time," boomed Mrs Weird. "Have some chips. Pass him the vinegar, Ott. Anyone thought to take Dad down some? No? I will, then."

And so saying, she gathered up a pile of chips in some newspaper and strode from the kitchen.

Pinchton was totally amazed. Did nobody understand how serious the situation was?

"Doesn't anybody understand?" he wailed. "This is a crisis! My parents' bedroom is full of broken ceiling ..."

"Pinch," said Ott.

"... and they're going to kill me and I know I deserve it because it's all my fault because I let you in and let you ..."

"*Pinch!*"

"What?"

"Relax," said Ott. "Gran will fix it, won't you, Gran?"

"Don't be stupid," said Pinchton, crossly. "You saw the state of the place. As if one person could deal with that. And I wish people would stop telling me to relax."

The House Plant reached out a gentle tendril and stroked his arm. He pushed it away.

"She will," insisted Ott. "She can fix anything. Can't you, Gran?"

Gran sucked her mouth in, thought for a moment, nodded briskly and said, "Mostly. Except for world peace, but that's difficult."

"What – you're a trained plasterer or something?" Pinchton felt his hopes rise. It was against all reason, of course. Nobody could repair the terrible damage that had been done to Number 15, Tidy Street. Not in just a few hours.

But even so – he felt more hopeful.

"Never you mind," said Gran. "I'm full of surprises, I am."

She bustled over to a door in the corner, threw it open and reached in. Pinchton had never noticed a cupboard there before. He couldn't see inside. It seemed really dark in there. When she emerged, she held an old-fashioned broom in one hand and an

old leather bag – rather like the sort doctors carry – in the other.

"I'll be a while," she said. "Don't leave Frankly under the tap any longer, he'll shrink. Keep an eye on them chips."

"Shall I come and help?" offered Pinchton.

"Why? You doubting I can do it on my own?"

Without waiting for an answer, she turned on her tiny foot and marched out the back door with a business-like air.

"Anyone fancy a game of cards?" said Ott.

"Don't be silly," said Pinchton.

"Why not? It'll calm you down. You worry too much. He does, doesn't he, Oliver?"

"Mmm," said Oliver, twanging away.

"You see? Oliver agrees. We'll play snap. Watch the chips."

Ott went to get the cards, Oliver wandered over to remove a very wet Frankly from the overflowing sink, and Pinchton found himself standing over the frying pan, frying chips just as Ott had asked him to.

Ten minutes later, Mrs Weird wandered back in. And five minutes after that, they were all sitting playing snap on the kitchen floor. Pinchton even found he was enjoying himself, even though he was sure that the world as he knew it was about to end.

Which was weird.

Chapter 7
The Primms Return

Mr and Mrs Primm had not had a very relaxed journey home. In fact, they had had an argument. By accident, somehow, Mr Primm had cut his thumb. Not very deeply, but enough to make a fuss and get blood on the seat of the car. He had also drunk an extra beer with Uncle Brian, which meant that Mrs Primm had to drive.

Because she was distracted by Mr Primm's accident, Mrs Primm had taken the wrong slip road and ended up on the wrong motorway going in the wrong direction, which added an extra 40 minutes to the journey. And the twins had been really annoying and the carrot cake hadn't been cooked properly in the middle. And the walk around the village had been chilly and the garden centre had been closed.

All in all, it hadn't been one of their more enjoyable trips.

"Pinchton?" called Mrs Primm, stepping into the hall. "Where are you? We're home!"

"I'm up here, Mother," called Pinchton, quickly turning off his PlayStation 2. "In my room. Copying out my homework. I'll be right down."

His voice sounded almost normal. It had nearly stopped wobbling. Nearly.

Downstairs, Mrs Primm walked into the kitchen. She stood pulling her gloves off, looking around with a critical air.

Everything was just as she had left it. It looked like Pinchton had cleared up after himself very nicely. The pansy still hung in pride of place. It looked a slightly paler pink than she remembered. Something to do with the light, perhaps, or maybe it needed a drop of water.

"Hello, Mother," said Pinchton, coming in. He was smiling and looked the perfect son. "How was your day?"

"I'm worn out," said Mrs Primm, shortly. "Your father cut his finger."

"Really? I'll put the kettle on, shall I?"

"Thank you, darling." Mrs Primm gave a grateful little sigh. "That would be lovely. How was your thing?"

"My what?"

"You know. The jumble thing."

"Oh! Yes, that. Um ... fine. Hello, Father. How was your day?"

Mr Primm came yawning into the kitchen looking rumpled and grumpy and holding his sore finger out carefully.

"I don't think he remembers," said Mrs Primm meanly.

"I'm going upstairs to change," Mr Primm told her, and stomped upstairs.

A moment or so later, there came a loud cry. Pinchton's stomach turned over. What was up?

But all was well. His father came striding back into the kitchen, with a big smile on his face, clutching the leather jacket to his chest.

"Look at this!" he shouted to his startled wife. "Look what was laid out on the bed!"

"Good gracious, dear, that's your old jacket, isn't it?"

"That's it all right. And the old photo album. Look, here's me on the bike. I was only talking about it this morning, remember? Where were they, son?"

"Up in the loft," admitted Pinchton. "We – I popped up there earlier."

His father was already trying the jacket on. Sadly, it was too small for him.

"Pinchton!" gasped his mother. "You know the floor's unsafe. You could have fallen through the ceiling or something!"

"I was looking for the jacket," said
Pinchton, calmly. He crossed his fingers
behind his back. "I wanted to make Father
happy."

70

"Well – I suppose it was a sweet thought. Take it off, Rodney, it's too small."

"I proposed to you in this jacket, darling," said Mr Primm. "Remember?"

"I remember," said Mrs Primm, going a bit pink and giving a little giggle. "Let me see the photo then. Oh my! Look at your hair, darling."

"And here's you, look, in that pink cardigan. When we first met."

They stood together, peering at the photos underneath the slightly too pale pansy.

They were calling each other "darling" again. Pinchton left them to it and went to watch TV.

Some time later, he lay in bed staring at the ceiling, thinking about the weird happenings of the day. The last part, most of all.

This is what had happened.

They were just finishing their third game of snap when Gran had come bustling back in and told Pinchton that it was all done, he could go home now, and the next time the stars told him to stay in bed, perhaps he might like to take notice.

So Pinchton had gone home. In fear and trembling, he had gone home ...

And found everything completely back to normal! It was as if none of it had ever happened. The kitchen was sparkling. The pansy was back in its hanging basket. There was no hole in the bedroom ceiling and his parents' bedroom was clean and tidy with smiling photos on the bedside table. The only clue that something strange had happened was his father's leather jacket and the photo album, both of which had been placed neatly on the bed.

Gran had fixed it. How? He hadn't a clue. Somehow, he didn't think he should ask.

It had been like waking from a horrible nightmare. And, best of all, his Roman gladiator homework was finished. It was all copied out in his best writing. He knew it was the best work he'd ever done.

One thing was for certain. The Weirds were even weirder than he had thought.

Were they aliens? Visitors from another universe? Had Gran used magic? Some form of hypnotism? Was he going crazy? What? There was no end to the questions.

And he still hadn't found out the mystery of the Thudding Thing.

Maybe tomorrow ...

Barrington Stoke would like to thank all its readers for commenting on the manuscript before publication and in particular:

Stephen Boden
Jill Brook
Sue Byrne
Oliver Cain
Scott Campbell
Naomi Clarke
Glen Coombs
Christopher Dancer
Ashley Deveson
Oliver Donovan
Rosalind Faulkner
Mrs J. Gooch
Alex Goulding
Martin Harries Batkin
Douglas Holmes
Jacob Jennings
Lily Joyce
Laurence King
Mrs Sally Leszczynski
Rebecca McCluskie
Ryan McMaster
Darren Milne

William Morrison
Neil Musk
Benn Parry
Zhana Paton
Rhiannon Payne
Sabah Rasul
Lydia Rouland Greenstone
Charlotte Salmon
Michael Shield
Bryony Smith
Margaret Smith
Justin Stevenson
Jennifer Stewart
Lorna Tordoff
Tom van den Berg
Josie van Es
Megan Williams
Rhianna Wingar
Simone Wingar
Callum Wood
Callum Woolgar
Stephen Woosey

Become a Consultant!

Would you like to give us feedback on our titles before they are published? Contact us at the email address below – we'd love to hear from you!

Email: info@barringtonstoke.co.uk
Website: www.barringtonstoke.co.uk